STOv

Bad Mousie

ILLUSTRATED by

TRIENTJA ENGELBRECHT

Bad Mousie

WRITTEN by   MARTHA DUDLEY

Childrens Press

Once upon a time there was a little girl named Donica who lived with her mommie and a black mousie. The mousie was very bad because no one taught him to be good.

He hid one of Donica's new mittens. He made little mud tracks all over the rug whenever he came in.

He threw all of Donnie's clean socks into the bathtub when it had water in it.

Donnie's mommie said, "Mousie, don't you know that nobody loves a bad mousie? That's why we don't want you to stay here with us anymore." And she took her broom and swept him out of the house.

"Now don't you come back until you learn to be a good mouse," she called after him. Then she closed the door and locked it.

But Bad Mousie waited until dark. Then he
crawled under the gate and crept through a crack
in the wall. And the next morning, there he was
again! And Donnie was glad to see him.

But Mousie was still bad.

He pulled the top off the powder can and spilled powder all over the rug.

He tangled Donnie's hair and scattered her ribbons on the floor.

He tipped over things and spilled cocoa, and orange juice, and
lots and lots of milk.

This made Mommie very angry, and she said, "Bad Mousie, I'm going to put you in a box and close it tight and throw it into my wash tub full of water." And she did.

But the box was only glued together, and the water softened the glue and the box fell apart. So Mousie swam up to the top and scrambled out. Then he shook the water out of his ears and he climbed the cellar stairs and squeezed under the door. And there he was again! And Donnie was glad to see him.

Next day Mousie was as bad as ever. He pulled
all the books out of the shelves.

He took Mommie's lipstick and drew pictures
of Donica all over the bathroom wall.

He tipped over the big laundry hamper.

Now Mommie was very, very angry. She said,
"Mousie, you are so very bad that I shall feed you
to the night owl."

So she took him and tied him with three white strings to the fence in the back yard. Then she put a yellow ribbon around his neck so that the owl could see him better in the dark and fly down and gobble him up.

But before the stars came out, the mouse wriggled and tugged and finally got his feet loose. Then he untangled his tail, and nibbled through the strings around his tummy.

He was free again, and he ran and hid all night
so the owl could not find him.

Next morning, he came back to the house and
climbed in at an open window. There he was again.
And Donnie was glad to see him.

But Mousie was still bad! The next time Mommie was away at the store, he built a castle of all the pots and pans.

He dumped the buttons out of the button box.
And then he found a bottle of shoe polish and
painted the floor white.

When Mommie came home and found the terrible mess he had made, she grabbed him by his little string tail and she pressed her lips together hard and thought and thought of a way to get rid of him. At last she decided to let the wind blow him away.

She got out her oldest umbrella and fastened Mousie to the handle with an old belt. Then she carried him up onto the roof and opened the umbrella so the wind could blow him off, right off into the sky.

The little mouse kicked and squeaked, but it did him no good, for soon the umbrella was sailing up, up over the tree tops. And Mousie was fastened to it.

After a while the umbrella drifted gently down onto a little pink cloud. Mousie managed to get himself unbuckled and he let the umbrella drift away. Then he lay down on the soft warm cloud to rest. He was really very lonely and he wished that he could go home to Donnie and Mommie and live with them.

"Maybe I could learn to be good," he thought.

All of a sudden it began to get cold and the cloud began to drip. Drip, drip, drop, drop, dripple, dropple; the cloud was changing into rain. Mousie was getting wetter and wetter. Soon there was no cloud to lie on, and down he tumbled with the rain drops.

Down, down, until he splashed into a muddy puddle.

Mousie was cold and wet and very unhappy. He had to swim and wade to get out of the big puddle.

Then he ran as fast as he could to Donnie's house. But before he crept under the door, guess what he did? He wiped his muddy little feet on the door mat so Mommie's rugs would stay clean.

When Donnie looked around, there he was
again!

"Donnie," said the mouse, "could you teach me to be a good mouse? I want to stay here where it's warm and cozy, and be your friend."

"I'll try to teach you," said Donnie.
"And I'll try to be good," said the mouse.

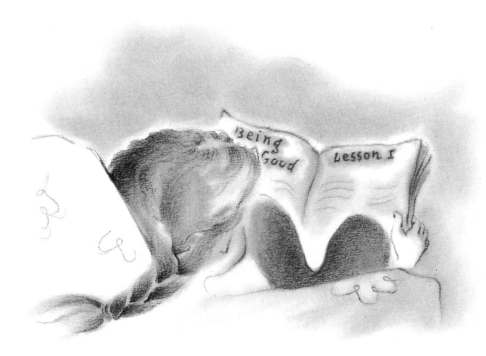

So Donnie taught him how to begin to be good.
She showed him what not to touch.

She taught him how to wipe up the milk he spilled.

She helped him to pick up the books and put the buttons away in the sewing box.

Then she kissed him to help him get good faster.

When Mommie came home from the store, she certainly was surprised, for there was Mousie helping Donnie set the table for lunch.

"Mommie, I'm teaching him to be a good mouse," said Donnie. "Mousie is trying very, very hard. Please let him stay. He can bring in the newspaper. He can wipe the forks and spoons. He can help me put my toys away."

So Mommie was proud of them both, and she told Mousie that she would help him learn to be good, too. Then she hugged Donnie and the mouse, and they all joined hands and danced around and 'round.

And they all lived cosily together.